WITHDRAWN

DINOSAURS DON'T HAVE BEDTIMES!

GR RR!

To Freddy and Lily,
with love
T. K.

For my beautiful big sister, Sarah,
who can only dream of sleep
N. D.

CANDLEWICK PRESS

DINOSAURS DON'T HAVE BEDTIMES!

Timothy Knapman illustrated by Nikki Dyson

"Dinnertime!" said Mommy.

"But dinosaurs don't *have* dinnertimes!" said Mo.

"Really?" said Mommy.
"They must get very hungry."
"They eat whenever they like," said Mo.

Gobble, Gobble, Crunch!

"And do they *always* make a terrible mess?"

"Yes!"

"Bath time!" said Mommy.

"But dinosaurs don't *have* bath times!" said Mo.
"They must have dirty ears!" said Mommy.

"Yes!" said Mo. "They roll around in the swampy water. They do not scrub beneath their claws. They don't put toothpaste on their jaws. They don't *want* to be clean and shiny!"

"Towel!"

"Pajama time!" said Mommy.

"But dinosaurs don't *wear* pajamas!" said Mo.

"They must get very cold!" said Mommy.
"Dinosaurs don't care!"
"Just the bottoms then," said Mommy.
"That is *not* fair!"

"Playtime!" said Mommy.

"Dinosaurs don't play nicely!" said Mo.

"They're much too big for that.
They wriggle and they run.
And they hide inside the jungle—
for days and days sometimes.
Then they jump out, shouting:
THAT'S dinosaur fun!"

"Milk time!" said Mommy.

"Dinosaurs don't drink their milk," said Mo.

"Dinosaurs rampage! They stomp around and knock things down."

STOMP!

Yaaaaawn!
"Bedtime!" said Mommy.
"Dinosaurs *don't* have bedtimes!" said Mo.

"They're never, ever tired."
"Don't they ever, ever sleep?"
"No!"

"But sometimes"—Mo yawned—
"They might just close their eyes.
And curl up tight and snuggle down.
But all of that's pretend."
"And do they get a good-night kiss?"
said Mommy.
"**Roar!** Roar!"

"SNORE..."

"Good night, dinosaur."